Baba's Gift

WRITTEN BY BEVERLEY AND MAYA NAIDOO

ILLUSTRATED BY KARIN LITTLEWOOD

PUFFIN BOOKS

For Ncumisa, Hlonela and Chumani ~ B.N. & M.N.

For Pablo ~ K.L.

Themba and Lindi live in South Africa, close to the Indian Ocean.
This is where Maya's dad grew up on a sugar cane farm
eating mealies (corn on the cob) and rotis (handmade flat round bread).

PUFFIN BOOKS

Published by the Penguin Group:
London, New York, Australia, Canada,
India, New Zealand and South Africa

Penguin Books Ltd, Registered Offices: 80 Strand, London WC2R 0RL, England

www.penguin.com

First published 2004

3 5 7 9 10 8 6 4 2

Text copyright © Beverley Naidoo and Maya Naidoo, 2004
Illustrations copyright © Karin Littlewood, 2004

Manufactured in China

ISBN 0–670–91184–4 Hardback
ISBN 0–140–56874–3 Paperback

Lindi and Themba got up with the sun.
Gogo was taking them to the sea for a day.
"I have work to do," said Baba, "but I have made
a present for you." It was a little wooden boat.

They walked through the
sugar cane fields to the bus stop.
"How big is the sea, Gogo?" asked Themba.

Gogo waved her arms.
"Bigger than all these fields!"
"Baba says we'll see boats bigger
than houses." Themba puffed out his chest.
"Our boat is very small," giggled Lindi.

"What a beautiful boat,"
admired a banana seller.
"We are taking it to
the sea for Baba,"
declared Themba.

"Hold it with this string,"
the man advised.
"Keep it safe!"

The bus raced over the hills. Sitting next to them was a
lady taking a hen to market. BUMP! The cage door
flew open. Lindi grabbed the bird and gave it back.

The lady gave them each a stick of sugar cane. "Where are you going?" she asked.

"To the sea," sang Lindi.

"To the sea!" echoed Themba. "We are going to sail Baba's boat."

"It's beautiful! Don't lose it!" warned the lady.

"Never!" Themba shook his head.

"We'll be careful!" Lindi promised.

The city was full of people pushing and shouting. They passed shops and stalls.

"Hold on to my hand!" called Gogo.

"Hold on to the boat!" Themba called to Lindi.

"I can see the sea, Gogo!" Themba pulled Gogo's hand.
"Slow down," she laughed. "I'm an old lady."

"We must put down this blanket," said Gogo. "Then I can sit and watch you."

A gust of wind caught the blanket and it billowed in the air.

"Let me help you," offered a lady with friendly eyes.

A girl skipped alongside her. "Do you want to play in the sea?"
she asked. "My name is Devi."

Themba and Lindi grinned.

"Watch out for the waves!" Gogo warned.

"Don't go too deep!" called Devi's mother.

"I can teach you a game." Devi hopped from one foot to the other.

"Stand here! Don't let the water touch your toes!"

"You touched the water!" yelled Themba.

"It's cold!" squealed Lindi, jumping up and down.

"Aaaaaah!" screamed Themba.

"Eeeeeeh!" shrieked Lindi.

"I like your boat!" shouted Devi.

"Our Baba made it," Lindi beamed.

"When he was little he worked on big boats."

"Let's sail it!" called Themba.

"Give me the string!"

They took it in turns
to pull the boat.
They watched it
bounce and swirl.

Suddenly a large
wave crashed into them.
It knocked Themba
over but he held
on to the string.

"No, you can't have Baba's boat!"
He made a fist at the sea.
Lindi and Devi both laughed.
"Come and eat!" Gogo's
voice floated over
the waves.

Themba put the boat next to
Gogo and clutched his tummy.
"I'm starving!"

"I could eat all the sugar cane in the world!" Lindi exclaimed.

"I could eat a big fat lion!" Devi boasted.

"Well, you can start with these mealies," laughed Gogo.

"And these rotis!" Devi's mother unpacked her basket.

"I'm full," groaned Themba.

"Come on, let's build a sand hut," said Lindi.

"But we don't have grass for the roof," complained Themba.

"We can use shells," said Devi. "I'll look for some while you build the walls."

"Let's make a river for the boat," Lindi suggested.

Themba and Devi dug a river. Lindi carried water from the sea.

But the water sank into the sand every time.

"It's the sand monsters!" Themba growled.

"They drink all the water."

Themba sprang to his feet.

"I'm a monster! I'm going to gobble you up!"

He chased Devi and Lindi along the beach.

Some children were playing football.

"Do you want to play?" asked a girl with flying hair.

They joined in the game.

No one saw the sea slowly

creeping up the sand.

They played until they were tired and Devi
kicked the ball into the water. "That's out, man!"
A boy waded in to fetch it.
The sea had sneaked up close.
"It's time to go, children!" called Gogo.
"Time to go home!"
Devi's mother pointed to her watch.

"See you next time!" Devi waved goodbye.

"Let's pack up quickly," said Gogo.

Themba was the first to remember.

"Oh no! Baba's boat!"

"We left it by the sand hut!" cried Lindi.

But the sea had washed over the hut.

They searched everywhere.

Themba ran along the beach,

sweeping his eyes from the sand to the sea.

"The sea has stolen Baba's boat!" Lindi wailed.

"It's late," insisted Gogo. "We have to go."

"But we can't go without it!" sobbed Lindi.

"Where is Themba?" Gogo looked worried.

She called his name. "I am here!" sang a little shadow.

"Look! I found a present for Baba!"

Themba held up a gleaming oyster shell.

"Ah! It's wonderful!" murmured Lindi.

The bus sped back through the night.

"Is Baba's boat at the bottom of the sea, Gogo?

Will he be angry?" Themba clutched the oyster shell.

"Baba's boat is strong. It will sail far away," Gogo promised.

"It will go to India," Lindi dreamed.

Themba and Lindi curled up with Gogo.

She was warm and smelled of the sea.

"Baba will love his shell," said Gogo softly.

The bus was quiet.

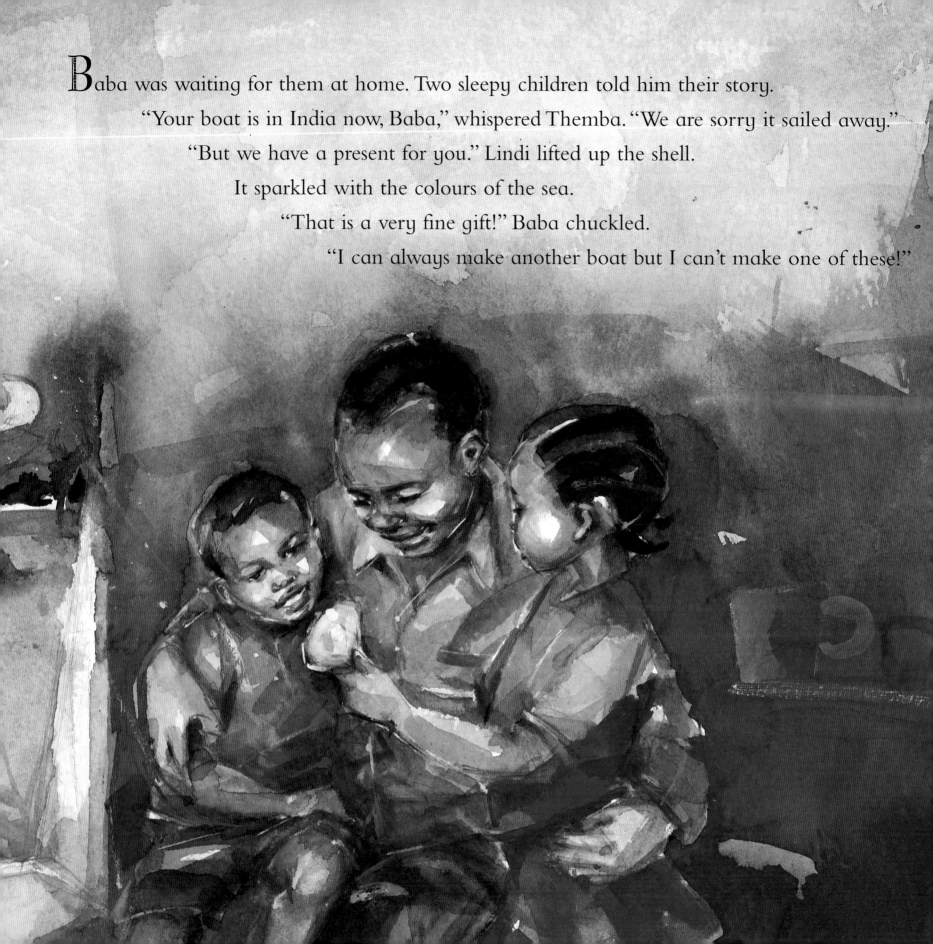

Baba was waiting for them at home. Two sleepy children told him their story.

"Your boat is in India now, Baba," whispered Themba. "We are sorry it sailed away."

"But we have a present for you." Lindi lifted up the shell.

It sparkled with the colours of the sea.

"That is a very fine gift!" Baba chuckled.

"I can always make another boat but I can't make one of these!"